## Dear Parent:

Remember the first time you read a book by yourself? I do.
I still remember the thrill of reading the words Little Bear said
to Mother Bear: "I have a new space helmet. I am going to
the moon."

Later when my daughter was
learning to read, her favorite I
Can Read books were the funny
ones—Danny playing with the
dinosaur he met at the museum
and Amelia Bedelia dressing
the chicken. And now as a new
teacher, she has joined the thou-
sands of teachers who use
I Can Read books in the classroom.

I'm delighted to share this commemorative edition with you.
This special volume includes the origin stories and early sketches
of many beloved I Can Read characters.

Here's to the next sixty years—and to all those beginning
readers who are about to embark on a lifetime of discovery that
starts with the magical words *"I can read!"*

**Kate M. Jackson**
Senior VP, Associate Publisher, Editor-in-Chief

*For stargazers everywhere*
*—J.O'C.*


*For Yarden and Yonatan,*
*who shine brightly in my heart*
*—R.P.G.*


*For the PA Stargazers,*
*whose friendship bends the Space/Time Continuum*
*—T.E.*

I Can Read Book® is a trademark of HarperCollins Publishers.

www.icanread.com

Library of Congress Cataloging-in-Publication Data

O'Connor, Jane.

Fancy Nancy sees stars / by Jane O'Connor ; cover illustration by Robin Preiss Glasser ; interior illustrations by Ted Enik. — 1st ed.

p.    cm. — (I can read book) (Fancy Nancy)

Summary: When a rainstorm prevents Nancy and her friend Robert from getting to the planetarium the night of a class field trip, she has a brilliant idea for making things better.

ISBN 978-0-06-257275-2

[1. Astronomy—Fiction.   2. School field trips—Fiction.   3. Planetariums—Fiction.]   I. Enik, Ted, ill.   II. Title.

PZ7.O222Fgs  2009                                                                                                2008010284

[E]—dc22                                                                                                                        CIP

AC

17  18  19  20  21    SCP    10  9  8  7  6  5  4  3  2  1    ❖    First Edition

# Fancy NANCY Sees Stars

by Jane O'Connor

cover illustration by Robin Preiss Glasser

interior illustrations by Ted Enik

**HARPER**

*An Imprint of HarperCollinsPublishers*

Stars are so fascinating.

(That's a fancy word

for interesting.)

I love how they sparkle in the sky.

Tonight is our class trip.

Yes! It's a class trip at night!

We are going to the planetarium.

That is a museum

about stars and planets.

Ms. Glass tells us,

"The show starts at eight.

We will all meet there."

I smile at my friend Robert.

My parents are taking Robert and me.

7

Then Ms. Glass asks,

"What star is closest to Earth?"

That's easy.

It's the sun.

"What do you call stars
that make a picture?"
asks Ms. Glass.
Robert and Bree have both forgotten.
"I know, I know," I say.
"A constellation."

Ms. Glass nods.

On the wall are pictures.

There's the hunter and the crab

and the Big Dipper.

It looks like a big spoon.

We will see all of them at the show.

I can hardly wait.

At home, Robert and I
put glow-in-the-dark stickers
on our T-shirts.
Mine has the Big Dipper.
Robert has the hunter on his.

We spin my mobile

and watch the planets orbit the sun.

(Orbit is a fancy word.

It means to travel in a circle.)

Then we pretend to orbit

until we get dizzy.

15

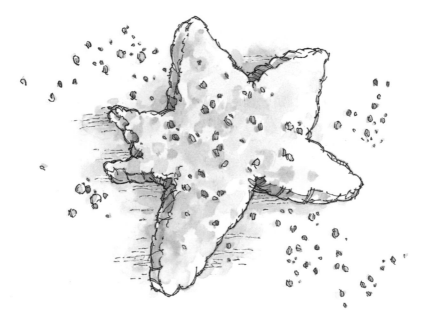

Later, we bake star cookies.

Sprinkles make them sparkle.

"The sun is a star,"

I tell my sister.

"It is the closest star,

so we see it in the day."

After dinner,

we wait for the baby-sitter.

She is very late.

Dad says not to worry.

We have plenty of time.

At last we get in the car.

Drip, drip, drip.

It is raining.

The rain comes down

harder and harder.

Dad drives slower and slower.

It is getting later and later.

A policeman comes over.

"The road is closed,"

he tells my parents.

"There is too much water."

Oh no!

There are cars in front of us.

There are cars behind us.

We are stuck!

"The show is starting soon!"

Robert says.

"We will not make it."

Drip, drip, drip goes the rain.

Drip, drip, drip go my tears.

Robert and I are so sad.

We do not even want any cookies.

At last the cars move

and the rain stops.

But it is too late.

The night sky show is over.

By the time we get home,

the sky is full of stars.

They are brilliant!

(That's a fancy word

for shiny and bright.)

I get a brilliant idea.

(Brilliant also means very smart.)

We can have

our own night sky show.

My parents get my sister.

We set up beach chairs.

Mom lights candles.

Dad puts the cookies on a tray.

We eat alfresco.

(That's fancy for eating outdoors.)

28

We watch the stars.

We see the North Star.

We see the Big Dipper.

All at once,

something zooms across the sky.

"A shooting star," Dad says.

"Make a wish!"

I tell Dad it is not a star.

It is a meteor.

But I make a wish anyway.

The next day Ms. Glass says,
"Everyone missed the show
because of the storm.
So we will go next week."
Everybody is very happy.
And guess what? My wish came true!

# Fancy Nancy's Fancy Words

## These are the fancy words in this book:

Alfresco—outside; eating outside is called eating alfresco

Brilliant—bright and shiny, or very, very smart

Constellation—a group of stars that makes a picture

Fascinating—very interesting

Meteor—a piece of a comet that leaves a blazing streak as it travels across the sky (you say it like this: me-tee-or)

Orbit—to circle around something

Planetarium—a museum about stars and planets

## "I can read! I can read! Where are the books for me?"

$\sim$

One question from a young reader sparked a reading revolution!

A conversation between the director of Harper's Department of Books for Boys and Girls, Ursula Nordstrom, and Boston Public Library's Virginia Haviland inspired the I Can Read book series. Haviland told Nordstrom that a young boy had burst into the children's reading room and asked her where he could find books that were just right for a brand-new reader like himself.

Determined to fill this gap, Nordstrom published *Little Bear* by Else Holmelund Minarik, with illustrations by Maurice Sendak, in the fall of 1957. The response was immediate. According to the *New York Times*, "One look at the illustrations and children will grab for it. A second look at the short, easy sentences, the repetition of words, and the beautiful type spacing, and children will know they can read it themselves."

Delightful and wonderfully warm, Little Bear served as the template for the series, and now, sixty years later, we have over four hundred I Can Read stories for our youngest and newest readers!

$\sim$

# Where the Ideas for the Characters Came From

### Berenstain Bears

Stan and Jan Berenstain were cartoonists in the 1950s. When their sons began to read, they submitted a story about a family of bears to author, editor, and publisher Ted Geisel (aka Dr. Seuss), which was published as *The Big Honey Hunt* in 1962. Geisel labeled their next effort "Another Adventure of the Berenstain Bears." That's how the bears got their name!

### Biscuit

One day while watching her daughter play with their neighbor's frisky dog, Alyssa Capucilli was struck by her daughter's patience and gentle nature, as well as the fact that her little girl thought the dog understood every word she said. That was the inspiration for the little yellow puppy and his sweet companion. Pat Schories's warm illustrations capture their tender relationship.

### Pete the Cat

When James Dean first saw Pete, he was a tiny black kitten in a shelter. Pete looked like he had been starved and his black fur was a mess. At first, James had no interest in Pete—black cats were bad luck, after all! But the scrawny little fellow stuck his paw out of the cage, wanting to play! James took Pete home. And even though James chose to paint Pete the Cat blue (his favorite color), James realizes now that black cats are actually very good luck.

### Danny and the Dinosaur

In 1958, cartoonist Syd Hoff's daughter Susan was going through a rough surgery, and one day, Syd decided to draw a picture to cheer her up. It showed a dinosaur with Syd's brother on its back. When Susie saw the picture, she exclaimed, "Danny and the dinosaur!" and that night after the family went to bed, Syd wrote the story.

## Pinkalicious

Victoria Kann's daughters could never seem to get enough of cupcakes or the color pink! One year, as an April Fools' joke, Victoria told her family and friends that one of her daughters had turned pink from eating too many pink cupcakes—and so the idea for *Pinkalicious* was born!

## Frog and Toad

The characters of Frog and his best friend, Toad, might have been inspired by . . . a horror movie! Arnold Lobel and his daughter, Adrianne, went to see a movie called *Frogs* at the drive-in. However, the movie featured not frogs, but toads! Adrianne told her dad about the many differences between the two—and two years later the first Frog and Toad book, *Frog and Toad Are Friends*, appeared.

## Little Critter

Mercer Mayer was doodling around one day in 1974 when he drew a shape like a gourd, put two eyes on it, scribbled a nose connecting the eyes, then got coffee and forgot about it! The next day, he noticed a small piece of paper on the floor. It was his gourd. He added fuzzy hair and a big mouth; short stubby arms and feet. Mercer had created a fuzzy little "woodchuck-y porcupine" thing that became Little Critter!

## Fancy Nancy

When Jane O'Connor was a small girl, every Sunday, when her grandma and great aunts came to visit, Jane would greet them at the door in a tutu and a pair of her mom's high heels. She thought she looked très glamorous!

Years later, while she was fixing dinner one night, the name Fancy Nancy flew into Jane's head, and a star made her debut!

## Amelia Bedelia

*Amelia Bedelia* was inspired by Peggy Parish's third-grade students at the Dalton School in New York City. The children mixed up words, and Parish found them hilarious. That gave Parish the idea for Amelia Bedelia—a character who takes every word literally and embraces life with an outlook that is forthright and optimistic. Illustrator Fritz Siebel worked with Parish to create the perfect look for the conscientious cleaning lady.

# Early Character Development

## The Berenstain Bears

Stan and Jan Berenstain's early sketches from *The Berenstain Bears Clean House*

## Pete the Cat

## Frog and Toad

Early character sketch of Frog and Toad

James Dean's first painting of Pete the Cat

JAMES DEAN
12. 26. 99

## Biscuit

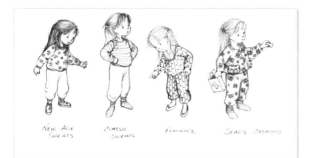

*Biscuit* character sketches

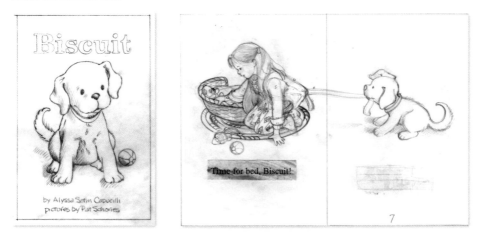

Pat Schories's early sketches from *Biscuit*

## Pinkalicious

Victoria Kann's sketches for the picture book *Pinkalicious*

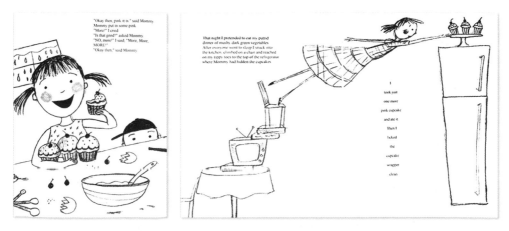

## Amelia Bedelia

Fritz Siebel's sketches
for the picture book
*Amelia Bedelia*

## Danny and the Dinosaur

Syd Hoff's early cover sketches for *Danny and the Dinosaur*

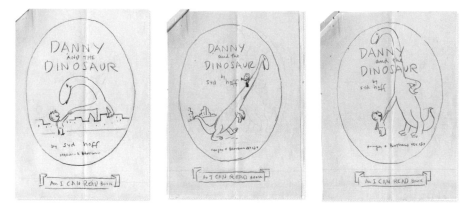

## Little Critter

Mercer Mayer's early
character sketches of
Little Critter

## Fancy Nancy

Robin Preiss Glasser's character sketches and cover sketch for *Fancy Nancy and the Boy from Paris*

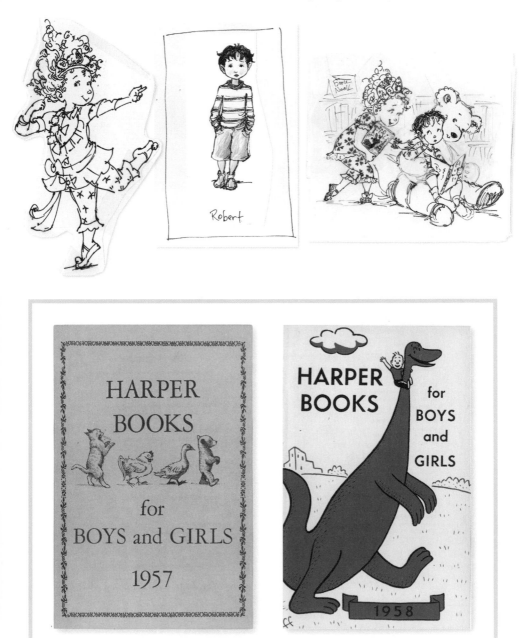

These two catalogs marked the launch of I Can Read!

# Sixty Years of I CAN READ

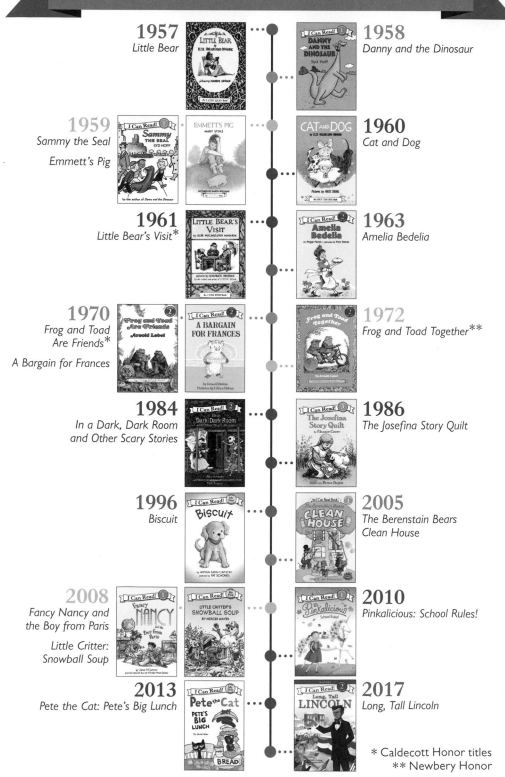

**1957**
Little Bear

**1958**
Danny and the Dinosaur

**1959**
Sammy the Seal

Emmett's Pig

**1960**
Cat and Dog

**1961**
Little Bear's Visit*

**1963**
Amelia Bedelia

**1970**
Frog and Toad
Are Friends*

A Bargain for Frances

**1972**
Frog and Toad Together**

**1984**
In a Dark, Dark Room
and Other Scary Stories

**1986**
The Josefina Story Quilt

**1996**
Biscuit

**2005**
The Berenstain Bears
Clean House

**2008**
Fancy Nancy and
the Boy from Paris

Little Critter:
Snowball Soup

**2010**
Pinkalicious: School Rules!

**2013**
Pete the Cat: Pete's Big Lunch

**2017**
Long, Tall Lincoln

\* Caldecott Honor titles
\*\* Newbery Honor